Exploring Spirituality with Your Child

Much has been written about the importance of reading simple, beautiful books to babies and preschoolers to stimulate brain development. But perhaps even more important, what you read begins to shape your child's world, and creates the images that will remain with him or her throughout life. We read books to our children about letters, numbers, shapes, colors and safety, but do we give their minds the early food they need to think about life's bigger questions?

As spiritual development experts now tell us, each child develops an image of God by age 5, with or without religious instruction. *I Am God's Paintbrush* takes you and your child on an imaginative journey designed to help you open not only your child's mind, but your child's heart and soul as well.

For Darwin and Ari, the new colors in my paintbox. —*SES*

Text © 2009 by Sandy Eisenberg Sasso
Illustrations © 2009 by SkyLight Paths Publishing

Library of Congress Cataloging-in-Publication Data is available upon request.

ISBN-13: 978-1-59473-265-2
ISBN-10: 1-59473-265-5

Walking Together, Finding the Way
SkyLight Paths® Publishing
www.skylightpaths.com

Green, purple,
red and white

All these colors—some **dark,** some light—

are God's colors painting our world.

Point to
the **colors**
you like
best.

Dad beats on the drum.
Mom sings and hums.

They are part of God's song.

When I laugh, when I cry,
I am part of God's song, too.

Sing with me your
favorite song.

Trees sway,

the wind blows.

All these movements—

fast and slow—

they are God
dancing.

When I twirl,
when I sing,
I am part of
God's dance, too.

Do you like to dance?

I close my eyes real tight.
I see green, purple, red and white.
I think these are God's colors.

I know
God's colors
are in me, too.

And I can paint with God's paintbrush.

More Award-Winning Board Books for You and Your Child to Share
• Endorsed by Protestant, Catholic, Jewish, and Buddhist Religious Leaders •
• Multicultural, Nondenominational, Nonsectarian •
• For ages 0–4 • 5 x 5 • 24 pp •

Adam & Eve's New Day
By Sandy Eisenberg Sasso
Full-color illus. by Joani Keller Rothenberg
With the first sunset, Adam and Eve learn how to get through the night and not be afraid of the dark.
ISBN: 978-1-59473-205-8

How Did the Animals Help God?
By Nancy Sohn Swartz
Full-color illus. by Melanie Hall
God asks all of nature to offer gifts to humankind—with the promise that the humans would care for creation in return.
ISBN: 978-1-59473-044-3

How Does God Make Things Happen?
By Lawrence and Karen Kushner
Full-color illus. by Dawn W. Majewski
A charming invitation for young children to explore how God makes things happen in our world.
ISBN: 978-1-893361-24-9

Naamah, Noah's Wife
By Sandy Eisenberg Sasso
Full-color illus. by Bethanne Andersen
When God tells Noah to bring the animals onto the ark, God also calls on Naamah to save each plant.
ISBN: 978-1-893361-56-0

What Does God Look Like?
By Lawrence and Karen Kushner
Full-color illus. by Dawn W. Majewski
A simple way for young children to explore the ways that we "see" God.
ISBN: 978-1-893361-23-2

What Is God's Name?
By Sandy Eisenberg Sasso
Full-color illus. by Phoebe Stone
Everyone and everything in the world has a name. What is God's name?
ISBN: 978-1-893361-10-2

Where Is God?
By Lawrence and Karen Kushner
Full-color illus. by Dawn W. Majewski
A gentle way for young children to explore how God is with us every day, in every way.
ISBN: 978-1-893361-17-1

Printed in the USA
CPSIA information can be obtained
at www.ICGtesting.com
JSHW072028140824
68134JS00044B/3838